Walter the Baker

For my mother and father

Walter the Baker

Eric Carle

Aladdin Paperbacks

Long ago, in a town encircled by a wall,
lived Walter the Baker, his wife Anna, and their son Walter Jr.

Walter the Baker was known even outside the walls of the town.
He was the best baker in the whole Duchy.
Early every morning, while everybody else was still asleep,
Walter began baking his breads, rolls, cookies, tarts, and pies.

Anna sold the baked goods in the store.
No one could resist the warm, sweet smells drifting from Walter's bakery.
People came from near and far.

The Duke and Duchess who ruled over the Duchy
loved Walter's sweet rolls.
Every morning Walter Jr. carried a basketful of warm sweet rolls
to the castle where they lived.

"Mm," said the Duchess, spreading quince jelly on her roll.
"Ahh," said the Duke, putting honey on his.
And so each day was the same as the day before—
until one early morning…

…when Walter's cat was chasing a mouse and tipped over the can of milk.
"What will I do?" cried Walter.
"I cannot make sweet rolls without fresh milk."
In desperation, Walter grabbed a pitcher of water.
"I hope nobody will notice the difference," he said
as he poured the water into the flour to make the dough.

Now, you and I may not be able to tell the difference between a roll made with water and one made with milk.
But the Duke and especially the Duchess could tell the difference.
"Ugh," cried the Duchess after she took a bite.
"What is this!" roared the Duke.
"Where is Walter the Baker? Bring him here at once!"

So Walter was brought before the Duke.
"What do you call this?" roared the Duke.
"This is not a roll, this is a stone!" And with that he threw it at Walter's feet.
"I used water instead of milk," Walter admitted, hanging his head in shame.
"Pack your things and leave this town and my Duchy forever,"
 shouted the Duke. "I never want to see you again!"
"My Duke," pleaded Walter, "this is my home. Where will I go?
 Please give me one more chance, please."

"I must banish you," said the Duke.
But then he remembered Walter's good rolls and how much he and the Duchess would miss them.
"Well, Walter…" the Duke started to say.
Then he thought and thought some more.
"You may stay if you can invent a roll through which the rising sun can shine three times."
And to make it more difficult, he added, "It must be made from one piece of dough, and most of all, it must taste good.
Now go home and bring me such a roll tomorrow morning."
Poor Walter! Worried and sad, he trudged back to his bakery.

Walter worked all day and into the night.
He made long rolls, short rolls, round rolls, twisted rolls.
He made thin rolls and he made fat rolls.
And he worked some more.

Walter beat, pulled, pushed, and pounded the dough.

But it was all in vain.

He could not come up with a roll that would please the Duke.
By early morning Walter had only one long piece of dough left.
"It's hopeless," he cried.
In a sudden fit of anger, he grabbed the last piece of dough
and flung it against the ceiling.
"Stick there!" he yelled at the dough.
But it didn't. It fell, twisting itself as it dropped down
and plopped into a pail of water.

Anna and Walter Jr. were awakened by Walter's yell and
rushed into the bakery just as Walter was about to dump out
the water and the twisted piece of dough.
"Father, stop!" shouted Walter Jr. "Look!"

And Anna quickly popped the dough into the hot oven.
Soon it was brown and crisp.
She took out the roll and handed it to Walter.
It hadn't risen very high, but it had three holes.

Walter held up the twisted roll and smiled.
He saw that the morning sun was shining through it three times.

Walter put the roll into a basket and rushed to the castle
to deliver his invention to the Duke and Duchess.
And they too saw the morning sun shine through it three times.
Then the Duke and Duchess each took a small bite.
Walter was afraid to look, because he had no idea how it would taste.
"Well done!" said the Duke.
"Perfect!" exclaimed the Duchess.
Both were glad that Walter would not have to be sent away.

And Walter too was happy that he could stay.

"Now, pray tell us, Walter. What do you call this?" asked the Duke.

"Uh, yes, pray us tell…" Walter stammered, as he tried to come up with a name.

"What was that? Pra… pre… pretzel?" said the Duke. "Pretzel it shall be.

From now on," he declared, "it shall be sweet rolls in the morning…"

"… and pretzels in the afternoon," said the Duchess.

Walter returned to his bakery and spent all day and night making pretzels.
The next morning there were baskets of pretzels outside the store for
the whole town to taste.
And a special basket of pretzels for the Duke and Duchess.
And a cheer went up for Walter the Pretzel Maker.

*The word pretzel comes from the Latin word bracchium, meaning "arm."
The pretzel was originally a simple bread eaten during Lent. Its shape is based
on an ancient position for prayer in which the arms were folded across
the chest and the hands were placed on opposite shoulders.*

I wish to thank my neighbor Robert Normand,
Bakery and Konditorei in Northampton, Massachusetts,
for his technical assistance.

First Aladdin Paperbacks edit on April 1998
Copyright © 1972, 1995 by Eric Carle
Aladdin Paperbacks
An imprint of Simon & Schuster Children's Publishing Division
1230 Avenue of the Americas
New York, NY 10020

Originally published in 1972 by Alfred A. Knopf.

Also available in a Simon & Schuster Books for Young Readers hardcover edition.

The text of this book was set in 14-point Schneidler.
The illustrations were done in collage.
Cover and title page lettering by Julian Waters.
Printed in Hong Kong
10 9 3 7 6

The Library of Congress has cataloged the hardcover edition as follows:
Carle, Eric.
Walter the baker / by Eric Carle ;
p.   cm.
Summary: By order of the Duke, Walter the baker must invent a
tasty roll through which the rising sun can shine three times.
ISBN 0-689-80078-9 (hc.)
[1. Bakers and bakeries—Fiction. 2. Pretzels—Fiction.] I. Title.
PZ7.C21476Waj   1995   [Fic]—dc20   94-32364   CIP   AC
ISBN 0-689-82088-7 (pbk.)